For Laurence
with love

Bernadette and the Lunch Bunch

[signature]

Bernadette
and the
Lunch Bunch

Susan Glickman

Second Story Press

Library and Archives Canada Cataloguing in Publication

Glickman, Susan, 1953-
Bernadette and the lunch bunch/ by Susan Glickman

ISBN 978-1-897187-51-7

I. Title.

PS8563.L49B47 2008   jC813'.54   C2008-904618-8

Edited by Yasemin Ucar
Copyedited by Julia Horel
Designed by Melissa Kaita
Cover and illustrations by Mélanie Allard

Printed and bound in Canada

First published in the USA in 2009

The author gratefully acknowledges the support of the Ontario Arts Council.

*Second Story Press gratefully acknowledges the support of the Ontario Arts Council and
the Canada Council for the Arts for our publishing program. We acknowledge
the financial support of the Government of Canada through the Book
Publishing Industry Development Program.*

ONTARIO ARTS COUNCIL
CONSEIL DES ARTS DE L'ONTARIO

Canada Council   Conseil des Arts
for the Arts   du Canada

Published by
SECOND STORY PRESS
20 Maud Street, Suite 401
Toronto, ON M5V 2M5
www.secondstorypress.ca

For Jesse and Rachel

Contents

1

The Worst Year Ever!

Everyone agreed that Bernadette Inez O'Brian Schwartz was a most unusual child. Her first word was "Why?" So was her second word, and her third. From the time she could sit in her high chair, she designed experiments to satisfy her curiosity. Which would fall faster, a bottle of milk or a ripe banana? Which would fly higher, frozen peas or fresh blueberries? Which would make a bigger noise when it hit the floor, a bowl of cereal or a cantaloupe?

Soon she was not only asking "Why?" but also "Why not?" If you could slide *down* the slide, why couldn't you slide *up*? Why does orange juice taste terrible if you drink it after you brush your teeth? And how come china dishes come out of the dishwasher dry while plastic dishes stay wet?

These questions came into her mind at all hours of the day and night. Most of the time people were too busy to answer her because they were on the phone with Grandma Louise, or cooking dinner, or trying to drive through traffic without getting killed by some idiot talking on a cell phone. So luckily for everyone, when she turned four Bernadette started attending Garden Road Elementary School. School was supposed to be a good place for asking questions and getting answers, although some of the questions Bernadette asked were not the kind her teacher could answer. For example, when she skinned her elbow, she asked, "Why does everyone like to pull off scabs even though it hurts?" and when the teacher read *The Pokey Little Puppy,* she asked, "Why do dogs' feet smell like popcorn?"

Bernadette was disappointed that her teacher didn't know all the answers, but she tried to be glad about going to Junior Kindergarten anyway. It was fun walking to school with her next-door neighbor Marcus and his dog Sammy—whose feet really did smell like popcorn—especially when she got to hold the leash and pretend that Sammy was her very own dog. Besides, Bernadette had known Marcus all her life, and he was usually a scaredy-cat. He always cried when he fell off his bike or dropped his Popsicle, so she figured that if *he* was brave enough to go to school, she would be too.

The next year Bernadette made a real friend. Jasmine was not a cousin, or a neighbor, or the child of her parents' friends; Jasmine was the first friend Bernadette picked all by herself. Jasmine had long black braids, knobby knees that were always covered with bruises, and a laugh that lit up the room. She wasn't afraid of anything or anybody, and she loved doing experiments just as much as Bernadette did. In Kindergarten they made a volcano out of baking powder and vinegar and hatched butterflies from cocoons. In Grade One they made sugar crystals climb up a string and convinced the teacher to let them keep a pet toad in the classroom. In Grade Two they discovered cooking and made a different kind of magical mystery food at each other's houses every Sunday for three entire months. And then, in the summer after Grade Two, Jasmine told Bernadette she had terrible news.

"My mother got an amazing job, Bernadette," she said.

"Isn't that good news?"

"It's good for her, but not so good for me. Her new job is in Montreal. We have to move."

"You're moving? When?"

"In August. Before Grade Three starts."

"No, Jasmine! You're not allowed to move, *ever*. You're my best friend, and my almost-twin, and we always do everything together."

"We'll still be best friends, Bernadette. My parents promised we could come back for holidays to visit, and you can come stay with us any time you want," said Jasmine, giving Bernadette a big hug.

Bernadette hugged her back, but she still felt sad. "It won't be the same, just seeing you on holidays."

"I know. I'll miss you so much. But we can be pen pals and invent a secret code so that nobody else can read our letters. That will be something special, won't it?"

"I don't want *special*. 'Special' is just another name for 'different,'" said Bernadette. "And things were perfect just the way they were! I like sitting next to you in class and cooking weird stuff with you on the weekends. I want to keep reading stories to your baby brother and sneaking into your big sister's room to try on her clothes. I don't want anything to change, ever!"

"I don't either," said Jasmine. "But my mom says life is all about change."

The girls still had time to play together over the summer holidays. Their mothers even took them out shopping one day to buy beautiful stationery and lots of stamps so they could be pen pals. And then POOF! Jasmine was gone. Grade Three would be starting soon and Bernadette was really worried. She was going to have Mrs. Hawthorn this year, and Mrs. Hawthorn was famous for being the strictest teacher at Garden Road Elementary School. How could she face the strictest teacher in the whole school without Jasmine sitting beside her?

Just two days before school started, when Bernadette thought things couldn't possibly get any worse, another terrible thing happened. Bernadette's mother said that now that she was in Grade Three, she was big enough to eat lunch at school every day. In Grade Two Bernadette had gone home for lunch three or four days a week, but now she would be stuck in school all day long with mean Mrs. Hawthorn and no Jasmine! Grade Three was definitely going to be the worst year *ever.*

Besides, Bernadette loved eating at home with her mother. At home, she got to eat her favorite foods: grilled cheese and tomato sandwiches, and hot cocoa, and ripe peaches. None of these things tasted as good when you brought them to school. Grilled cheese sandwiches became cold and slimy, cocoa turned into boring old chocolate milk, and peaches got squished. There was an art to packing a lunch box and Bernadette Inez O'Brian Schwartz, the girl who usually wanted to know everything about everything, did NOT want to learn it.

Sometimes Bernadette's father came home for lunch, and if she ate at school, she'd miss out on that too. On the days that her father came home, Bernadette would set the table with placemats and matching napkins and they would all talk about their mornings at school and at work. Once, on her birthday, her family went out to lunch in a restaurant! When they finished eating their pizza, the manager of the restaurant gave her a brownie with a candle in it, and after she blew out the candle, Bernadette picked a prize from a big glass jar. She got a tiny blue notebook attached to a silver key chain, which was extremely cool, and useful as well.

But Bernadette wasn't little any more, so from now on, she would have to eat her lunch at school every single day.

"It's not fair!" she whined. "Everybody but me gets to go home for lunch."

"That's not true, Bernadette, and you know it," said her mother. "Lots of kids stay at school to eat. In fact, lunchtime is the best time to make new friends. There are all kinds of great activities then! There's basketball..."

"It's only for Grade Four and up."

"Newspaper club..."

"You have to be in Grade Five or Six."

"The chess team, the Save-the-Earth group, art lessons..."

"Nope, nope, and nope. All the good stuff is for the big kids."

"Well, that certainly doesn't seem fair. Do you want me to talk to the principal about it?"

"No, because that's not the reason I don't want to eat at school."

"Well, what *is* the reason then, Bernadette?"

"There are a lot of reasons. The lunchroom is

a total ZOO. Every time I have to eat there I feel sick. The tables are gross and sticky and there's even food on the floor. The teachers are always sending people to the principal's office for misbehaving. And they make us eat quickly so that they can use the lunchroom for other activities. Whenever I eat at school, I never have time to finish my lunch. In fact, that's probably why I'm so short. My growth is stunted from too many school lunches."

"Nice try, munchkin, but that doesn't explain why Daddy and I are short also, does it? I'm sorry, but there's just no choice. You have to eat at school because I have to work really hard this year."

"Can't you work really hard before and after lunch?"

"That doesn't give me enough time. And you are definitely old enough to manage a whole day at school by yourself."

"No, I'm not!"

"Yes, you are."

"NO, I'M NOT! And anyway, I don't WANT to."

"We can't always get what we want. I want a big backyard full of fruit trees, and my own private waterfall, and a guinea pig that doesn't shed, and a one-woman show at the art gallery. But those things aren't happening either."

"Ha, ha, very funny," replied Bernadette, in a very *un*funny tone of voice. When her mother started saying things like "We can't always get what we want," she knew there was no point arguing. It was game over.

On the first day of school, Bernadette refused to put on her new jeans, even though she had begged and begged for them and they were kind of expensive. She wore grubby old sneakers instead of her purple summer sandals, and a sparkly T-shirt Jasmine had given her for her seventh birthday that was really too small on her. She wanted to use her old knapsack too, but the zipper was broken and things kept falling out, so her mother wouldn't let her.

"I'm going to pretend it's still last year," she said. "Otherwise, this is going to be the worst year *ever*!"

"Do you really want to go back to Grade Two, Bernadette? In Grade Two you were the shortest kid in the class."

"Except for Annie Wang. And I'll bet I'm still the second-shortest kid in the class, just wait and see."

"And in Grade Two you didn't like the books the teacher read out loud; you said they were for babies," her mother continued.

"They were!"

"And in Grade Two you never got to do any real science projects, but Mrs. Hawthorn is famous for giving the Grade Threes amazing science projects."

"She's more famous for being strict."

"Bernadette Inez O'Brian Schwartz! If you start the year with a bad attitude you'll jinx yourself."

"I'm already jinxed, Mom. It's hopeless."

"But Grade Three will be great, Bernadette," Marcus said, when she told him she didn't want to go to school this year. "You get to do way more stuff than you did when you were little."

"Ha! Like what?"

"Like ball hockey," said Marcus. "And drama. And track and field."

"I don't want to do any of those things," said Bernadette. "I just want to be in the science fair."

"Yeah, that's pretty cool."

"If there wasn't a science fair to look forward to, I would probably just stay home and sit in the corner all by myself."

"Don't be such a crybaby," said Marcus. "Anyhow, I've got to go. Daniel's waiting for me to walk to school with him."

"Why are you walking with Daniel? What about me? You always walk to school with me, Marcus."

"You're a girl, Bernadette. I don't play with girls anymore. Sorry."

2

Bernadette has the Blues

Because it was only the first day of school and Bernadette was so worried, her mother agreed that she could come home for lunch.

"Good," Bernadette said. "I'll only have to last for two and half hours, and then I can have a nervous breakdown in the privacy of my own room."

"What's going on?" asked Marcus's mother.

"Bernadette has the blues," said Bernadette's mother.

"What does *that* mean?" asked Bernadette.

"It means that you're sad."

"I don't get it," said Bernadette. "What's sad about the color blue? The sky is blue, and it's not sad. The swimming pool at the community center is blue, and it's not sad. Blue jays are definitely not sad. My best party dress is blue, and it makes me happy!"

"It's just an expression."

"It's a silly expression. It doesn't make any SENSE!"

"Not everything has to make sense," said Bernadette's mother.

"Yes, it does!" shouted Bernadette. "And that's why I'm going to be a scientist. To explain *everything* to *everybody*."

"Bernadette Inez O'Brian Schwartz," said her mother. "Please stop making such a fuss. You're giving me a headache."

Bernadette's mother only called her by all four names when she was trying to be serious, but a lot of other people called Bernadette by all four names even when they were not. Probably it was because she was such a small girl that her name seemed longer than she was! Bernadette herself didn't mind, because she liked things to be absolutely clear. She wanted people to know exactly who she was, and she wanted to know as much as possible about the world around her. Some day she was going to write her *own* explanation of things, and it would actually make sense! She would call it **Bernadette's Guide to Everything Important.** She expected to win the Nobel Prize for it.

But first she had to get through Grade Three. No; first she had to get through the first *day* of Grade Three. All the way to school her mother chatted with Marcus's mother and Marcus walked ahead with Daniel. The boys were both in the other Grade Three classroom anyway, so even if she had walked to school with them, it wouldn't have made things any easier when they actually got there. At least Bernadette got to walk Sammy, which made her happy at first. But he kept pulling on the leash, wanting to keep up with the boys.

"Even the dog doesn't want to be friends with me anymore," she thought.

When they got to school, all the kids were yelling and screaming and hugging each other. Bernadette just stood by herself holding Sammy's leash while Marcus carried the dog around the yard to say hi to his friends. She stared at the ground and practiced being invisible until the principal, Mrs. Garcia, called out "Welcome to Garden Road Elementary School, boys and girls. It's time for all of you to line up and go to your new classrooms!" Then her mother finally stopped talking to the other parents and came over to say goodbye.

"I'm doomed," Bernadette groaned.

"Hang in there, Bernadette," her mother replied. "I have faith in you." And she turned around and walked across the playground without turning around to wave or to blow Bernadette a kiss.

Maybe I shouldn't go home for lunch today after all, Bernadette thought to herself. *Maybe I should just run away forever.*

"Hi, Bernadette," said a voice beside her. It was Annie Wang, who was famous for doing back walkovers in the schoolyard and for being even shorter than Bernadette. She had perfectly straight, black bangs as shiny as licorice and a shy smile with a missing tooth in it.

"Hi, Annie."

"I'm in Mrs. Hawthorn's class this year. Are you?"

"Yes. Unfortunately."

"Well, my big brother Michael had her when he was in Grade Three, and he liked her a lot," Annie said. "They went on field trips to the museum and the beach and stuff like that. And he made a kite that really flies. It'll be fun, you'll see."

"I hope you're right," said Bernadette. "But

I still think this is going to be the worst year ever."

They walked into the classroom, and the teacher was standing there to greet them.

"Welcome to Grade Three," said Mrs. Hawthorn. She was kind of old, and kind of fat, and wore glasses on a chain around her neck. "Every desk has a name on it. Find yours quickly and quietly, and sit down please."

Bernadette's desk wasn't even next to Annie's. Instead, she had to sit beside a skinny, blond boy named Jackie Renfrew, who was possibly the most annoying kid at Garden Road Elementary School. Once all the children were seated, Mrs. Hawthorn handed out books and told them to read the very first story and answer the questions that followed it. That was to test their reading comprehension. Then they had to do some arithmetic problems so that she could see how much they remembered from last year. It was all pretty easy for Bernadette, who was used to doing well in school, but it wasn't easy for Jackie Renfrew. He never understood the instructions the first time, so Mrs. Hawthorn had to repeat everything for him. Then he kept asking Bernadette to help him, especially with the arithmetic. And even when he understood what to do, his work was a mess. His handwriting started off big and got smaller and smaller and it was smudged and full of spelling mistakes. He was in tears by the time the lunch bell rang. Bernadette almost felt worse for him than she did for herself. Almost, but not quite.

"How was your morning, Bernadette?" asked her mother, who was waiting in the schoolyard.

"I don't want to talk about it," said Bernadette. And she didn't talk about it. In fact, she didn't talk at all. She just trudged home silently, and ate her grilled cheese and tomato sandwich silently. Then she lay on her bed pretending to read a book about fossils until it was time to go back to school. Her mom could tell she was serious about not talking, so she left her alone. But just before she said goodbye to Bernadette, she gave her a little silver box wrapped with a red ribbon.

"A surprise for recess," she said.

As soon as her mother was gone Bernadette peeked inside the box. She sort of knew what to expect because a very good smell was floating up from it, but she just had to make sure.

"What's that?" Jackie asked, as they lined up to go into the classroom.

"A chocolate cupcake for recess snack."

"You're lucky. I just have some cherries."

"I *love* cherries!" said Bernadette.

"I'll trade you," Jackie said.

"Maybe," said Bernadette. "If I'm still alive by recess."

In fact, the afternoon of the first day of Grade Three was a lot better than the morning because they had a real science lesson! Mrs. Hawthorn hung a prism of clear glass in the window to teach them all about the properties of light. When a sunbeam passed through the prism, beautiful colors shone out of it, sparkling and swaying over all the desks and chairs. The colors disappeared

when a cloud passed by, and then came back a few minutes later in shimmering waves of red, orange, yellow, green, blue, indigo, and violet.

"Wow!" said a bunch of the kids.

Jackie asked if he could take down the prism and examine it to see if there was some kind of magic trick involved. But there was no magic trick.

"What you are seeing is the true nature of light," explained Mrs. Hawthorn. "It really *has* all these different colors in it, but when they blend together in the air, they look clear. We can't see the hidden colors until we split the light beam by passing it through a prism. Where else do we see these very same colors in the very same order? Can anybody think of another place?"

"A rainbow?" asked Bernadette.

"Exactly!" said Mrs. Hawthorn. "The same thing happens to light when it passes through water drops in the air after a rainstorm. Good thinking, Bernadette."

Then a mean boy who was sitting behind her punched Bernadette on the shoulder and called her a show-off, so Mrs. Hawthorn made him apologize and stay in for recess to erase the blackboard and empty the wastebasket. Bernadette was happy the mean boy got punished; sometimes having a strict teacher wasn't such a bad thing after all! She was even happier thinking about those secret colors living inside each sunbeam and each drop of water. In fact, she was *so* happy that she gave annoying Jackie Renfrew half her cupcake for half his cherries.

In Kindergarten, Bernadette's class had spent a lot of time cutting things with really dull scissors, and pasting things with glue that didn't stick, and coloring boring pictures of animals with big eyes. Grade One was mostly about copying letters and numbers as neatly as possible, and lining up, and being quiet. Too much of Grade Two had been spent discussing the consequences of bad behavior, and having spelling tests. But a tiny part of her was starting to think Grade Three might just be OK after all, if Mrs. Hawthorn kept on teaching science!

When her mother picked her up after school, Bernadette forgot she was supposed to be mad at her and told her all about the experiment with light. Bernadette's mother said she was pretty sure there was a prism somewhere in their house, and that Bernadette could have it. As soon as they got home she went rummaging around in her studio and found it. They hung the prism in Bernadette's bedroom window and all the secret colors made a beautiful rainbow pattern across her desk. Bernadette put her hand into the rainbow, and the colors danced across it too.

"Look Mom," she said. "I really do have the blues! And the reds! And the yellows!"

"You certainly do, Bernadette," said her mother. "You have it all."

3

14, 15
19, 3, 9, 5, 14, 3, 5
6, 1, 9, 18

Sometimes Mrs. Hawthorn was kind of bossy. She had a very precise schedule the class had to follow, and lots of rules for how the students should behave in every possible situation. She had rules for waiting in line, and rules for sitting in class, and rules for writing on the blackboard. She had rules for handing in homework, or taking books out of the library, or even hanging up coats. But even though Bernadette was a little afraid of her teacher she could see that, in some ways, Mrs.

Hawthorn was just like her. They both liked things to be where they expected them to be and people to do what they expected them to do. Both of them were what Bernadette's mother called "highly organized."

For example, Bernadette had a lot of collections, and each one was stored in its own special container. She had a box for her rock collection and an album for stamps from around the world. She had a shiny biscuit tin for her model animals and a three-story-high glass cabinet for the tiny teapots that had belonged to her mother when she was a little girl. Bernadette kept pens, pencils, markers, and erasers in the middle drawer of her desk, white paper in the left-hand drawer, and colored paper in the right-hand drawer.

So she appreciated the way Mrs. Hawthorn organized the classroom. At the front of the room there was a zippy electric pencil sharpener, and at the back of the room there was a quiet library corner. These were two of Bernadette's favorite areas to visit. She also liked growing tomatoes in the little glass greenhouse and feeding the black and white striped angelfish in the big glass aquarium. The red flakes of fish food floating on the water didn't look anything like a tasty meal to Bernadette. But they must have tasted pretty good to the angelfish because they attacked those flakes like a bunch of kids running to a table for birthday cake.

The angelfish really loved lunchtime. But Bernadette hated it.

The first week of school lunches was terrible. Jackie Renfrew kept sitting beside her and wanting to trade whatever was in his lunchbox for whatever was in hers: pretzels and cheese for carrots and dip, apples for strawberries, pudding for yogurt. Bernadette's mother gave her a paper napkin with a different funny cartoon drawn on it every single day, but Bernadette refused to laugh. She took one bite out of her sandwich, one bite out of her cookie, and one bite out of her fruit. Then she left everything in her lunch box along with the crumpled-up napkin so that her mother would get the message.

The second week of school lunches was even worse. She didn't want to sit with Jackie anymore, but the kids at the new table were even more annoying than he was. On Monday somebody shoved her and she spilled orange juice all over her jeans. On Thursday somebody else pushed her chair, and she dropped her tuna sandwich on the floor. And on Friday, Mrs. Hawthorn gave everyone sitting there a detention—even Bernadette, who had been as quiet as a mouse.

Bernadette had noticed a group of Grade Three girls laughing and talking at a third table. She wished she could sit there, but worried that they wouldn't want her to join them. The only one Bernadette really knew was Annie Wang. Annie usually brought a big meal of soup or rice and vegetables to school and heated it up in the micro-wave. Bernadette loved to watch her eat because she never ever spilled even one tiny grain of rice, and she always peeled a tangerine for dessert and then put the peel back together so it looked like a whole fruit.

Bernadette told her mother about Annie's tangerines.

"That's exactly how I feel," she said. "I look like a whole kid on the outside, but the inside is missing. I miss Jasmine so much, Mom. I *told* you this was going to be the worst year ever, and I was right."

"Maybe you should ask Annie if you can sit with her," Bernadette's mother suggested.

"She already has friends to sit with and I don't know them," said Bernadette.

"Change always seems hard, Sweetie," said her mother, giving her a hug.

"It doesn't just seem hard, it *is* hard, Mom."

"Not for you, Bernadette. You've only been in Grade Three for two weeks, and things have already gotten better. Don't forget, you thought you were going to hate Mrs. Hawthorn, but instead you like her."

"I don't exactly *like* her. She's way too strict! I just like the fact that she teaches us real science, because I need to practice so that I can win the science fair."

Just before the winter holiday, Garden Road Elementary School always had a big science fair for Grades Three to Six. There were displays in the gym and prizes given by judges from the university, and the winner got to represent the school in the big city-wide competition in the spring. Ever since Grade One, Bernadette and Jasmine had been discussing what experiment they should do when they were finally old enough to participate. Now Jasmine wasn't here to be her partner, but Bernadette was still determined to enter the science fair on her own. And she was determined to win.

The next day Bernadette decided that she should start looking for a good experiment to do. Bernadette's mother said she wasn't allowed to experiment with electricity, or make anything that EXPLODED, which was kind of disappointing, but there were still a lot of other possibilities. A book of experiments in the school library had some interesting ideas, like measuring whether a dog's mouth or a human's mouth had more bacteria, or seeing how polluting water with detergent affected the growth of plants, or measuring the greenhouse effect by heating air under a glass jar. Then she found it: an absolutely perfect experiment! Bernadette was so excited she just had to tell Mrs. Hawthorn.

"Mrs. Hawthorn," she said, "I've been thinking

a lot about what experiment I should do for the science fair this year. I like cooking, so I want to do something that involves food. And you know how you split light with a prism to make all those colors come out? Well, I read that if you wet a Smartie and put it on a piece of blotting paper, you can make lots different colors come out of it, not just the one special color of the candy coating. Isn't that cool?"

"That's a great idea, Bernadette, but I'm afraid you'll have to hold onto it until next year," her teacher replied. "Or if you prefer, I'd be happy to do it in class."

"What do you mean?" asked Bernadette. "I don't want to do my experiment in class. I want to do it for the *science fair*!"

"Unfortunately a Grade Three student from another school got burned doing an experiment at the city finals last year and as a result, the school board has decided that the science fair should be restricted to Grades Four to Six from now on."

At first Bernadette was too shocked to say anything at all. Then a single tear slid down her face, right into her mouth. Bernadette licked the salty tear away quickly, hoping her teacher didn't notice.

"I don't believe this!" Bernadette said, in as angry a voice as she could manage. "*All* the good stuff is for the big kids. They already have the chess club, the newspaper club, the basketball team, and even the Save-the-Earth group. Who decided that you have to be in Grade Four to save the earth? That's the dumbest thing I've ever heard—except for keeping Grade Threes out of the science fair!"

"I understand how you feel, Bernadette, but I don't make the rules," said Mrs. Hawthorn, with a kinder voice than usual. "I'm sorry you're so disappointed."

As soon as Bernadette saw her mother in the schoolyard she really started to cry. "I told you this was going to be the worst year ever, and I was *so* right!"

"What happened now, Bernadette?"

"Some stupid kid got burned last year at the science fair city finals, so the school board decided that the science fair is too dangerous for Grade Threes. But being in the science fair is the only thing I was looking forward to this whole entire terrible year."

"Oh dear, that really is unfortunate," said her mother sympathetically.

"It's more than *unfortunate*," said Bernadette. "It's completely *unfair*! I even asked the principal if I could make an experiment just for our own private Garden Road Elementary School Science Fair, even if I couldn't compete for a spot in the city-wide competition. But she said that she wasn't allowed to make an exception for one student. She said that we all have to follow the rules even if we don't agree with them. I hate her, Mom. And I hate Mrs. Hawthorn. And I hate Grade Three!"

"Come on, Bernadette," said her mother, running her fingers through Bernadette's tangled curls. "Just be patient. It's only one more year until the science fair. Hey, I know what you can do—you can do some practice experiments in the meantime so that you'll have something truly amazing ready when you're allowed to enter it. What do you think of that idea?"

Bernadette didn't answer her, because she was so mad. Why did all the adults keep telling her she had to be patient? Why did they keep saying that next year's science fair was only a year away, as though that was really soon? A year was *not* soon. A year was as distant as Africa, as impossible as breathing underwater, as lonely as an empty house. How was Bernadette Inez O'Brian Schwartz—who not only wanted to be a scientist when she grew up, but knew she had been a scientist since the day she was born—supposed to wait a whole entire *year*?

The house was strangely calm for the next two weeks. Instead of telling her mother about everything that happened at school as soon as she came home each day, Bernadette just sat stroking her guinea pig, Hamlet, and staring out the window. At dinner she did not experiment by adding baking soda to her milk or food coloring to her mashed potatoes. In the bath she did not experiment by mixing together three kinds of shampoo, two kinds of shower gel and her father's shaving cream. Even in class, she no longer raised her hand to answer every single question about every single subject. And then she began to notice things, funny things, *surprising* things—things she'd never ever noticed before. So she wrote them down in a little green notebook in the special code she and

Jasmine made up to use as pen pals. She planned to send these notes to Jasmine eventually, but in the meantime, nobody else could read what she was writing.

This is how the secret code worked. You had to write out the whole alphabet at the top of the page and then all the numbers from one to twenty-six below it so you could substitute numbers for letters. A became the number 1, B became 2, C became 3, and so on; it took a lot of concentration to get everything right! In fact, because she was concentrating so hard, Bernadette sometimes missed what was going on around her in the classroom. Mrs. Hawthorn started getting impatient with her.

"Bernadette Inez O'Brian Schwartz," she said.

Bernadette thought to herself, *It is a disadvantage to have four names when people are angry, because they get to yell at you twice as long.* She started to write this observation down in her notebook, but the sentence was way too long and complicated to translate into number code, so instead she just wrote *6, 15, 21, 18 14, 1, 13, 5, 19.*

"BERNADETTE INEZ O'BRIAN SCHWARTZ!" Mrs. Hawthorn repeated, loudly.

Bernadette was about to put her notebook away when another thought occurred to her: *Sometimes when people talk, you can actually hear the capital letters.* She quickly wrote *2, 9, 7 14, 15, 9, 19, 5* in her notebook, closed it and pushed it aside.

But a few minutes later, when the teacher's back was turned, Bernadette was at it again. Unfortunately, Mrs. Hawthorn seemed to have eyes in the back of her head and without even turning around she ordered, "Put away that notebook and get out your math homework this instant!"

Teachers always tell you to be polite, but they never say 'please' themselves, Bernadette observed. She hastily scribbled *2, 1, 4 20, 5, 1, 3, 8, 5, 18!*

before slamming her notebook shut and cramming it into her desk.

This was definitely, positively, going to be the worst year ever.

4

The Lunch Bunch

After the first month of Grade Three, Bernadette decided things couldn't get any worse. Jasmine was gone, and now she didn't even have the science fair to look forward to. She was still sitting beside annoying Jackie Renfrew in the classroom and with a bunch of noisy, troublemaking kids in the lunchroom. So, figuring that she had nothing to lose, Bernadette took a deep breath and walked over to where Annie was sitting with two other girls from their class, Megan MacDonald and Keisha Clark. They were both tall and pretty, and sang in the school choir. They always wore the latest fashions. Keisha even had her ears pierced and sometimes wore sparkly lip-gloss to school. Bernadette wasn't really sure she liked these girls, but her mother always said, "You can't judge a book by its cover," and everyone always says you should listen to your mother. And besides, *nothing* could be as bad as getting another detention.

"Hi Bernadette. Do you want to sit with us?" Annie asked immediately, before Bernadette could even say one word.

"Yes, please! It's way too noisy back there," Bernadette replied gratefully.

"We were wondering how you could stand it," said Megan. "Are you eating lunch at school every day now?"

"Uh huh. I *hate* it," said Bernadette.

"It's not so bad if you sit with your friends," said Keisha.

"I would, but I don't know many people. I always did everything with my best friend, Jasmine Chatterjee, but she moved away this summer. I miss her so much!"

"I remember her," said Annie. "She had really long hair, and she laughed a lot. And she was the fastest runner in our grade. But Bernadette, you must have some other friends beside Jasmine."

"Not really," said Bernadette. "Except for Marcus, who lives next door. But he won't even walk to school with me anymore, because he's decided that it's not cool to play with girls."

"No wonder you look so lonely," said Megan kindly. "We can be your new friends, Bernadette. It's better to have more than one friend anyway. You should have a whole bunch."

"A Lunch Bunch!" said Bernadette, laughing.

"That's a great name for us," said Annie. "We could be a special sort of club."

"A club that just eats lunch together?" said Keisha. "That's not very exciting. We need more activities than that, you guys."

"We could invent strategies to make lunchtime exciting," said Bernadette.

"Like what?" wondered Annie.

"Well...we could have an Exotic Fruit Week, where we each try to bring a fruit we've never eaten before. Or a Hot Lunch Week, where every single day we bring real food like Annie does, and heat it up in the microwave."

"That sounds like fun!" said Megan.

"Or here's a good one," continued Bernadette. "How about a Color Day?"

"What's a Color Day?" asked Keisha.

"On a Color Day, all the food in your lunchbox has to match. For example, on an Orange Day, you could bring macaroni and cheese and an orange, or on a Red Day you could bring tomato soup and cherries."

"That's a great idea, Bernadette!" said Annie. "Some colors would be really hard, though. How could you do a Blue Day?"

"I don't know. We could try it, and see what we come up with," Bernadette replied.

"Maybe we should start with an easy one for practice," Keisha suggested. "And since Bernadette invented the strategy, she should get to pick first."

"Actually, I wish every day was a Brown Day," said Bernadette. "Then I could bring a totally chocolate lunch!"

"Well, since you started the Lunch Bunch," said Annie, "tomorrow can be a Brown Day in your honor."

As soon as Bernadette got home from school she raided the fridge. What could she bring for a brown lunch? They weren't allowed to bring peanut butter sandwiches because some kids in school were allergic to peanuts. And she was already getting sick of tuna, which wasn't really brown anyway, but sort of a pinky-beige. When you started really thinking about color, things turned out to be hard to classify. Most fruits were different inside and out. Everyone said that apples were red and bananas were yellow, but inside both were white. Blueberries weren't really blue, they were more like purple, and inside they were green. Some orange juice was yellow. Red lettuce was mostly green. Red cabbage was purple.

Bernadette stood there for so long with the fridge open that her mother came into the kitchen to see what was going on.

"Brrrrrr. There's an arctic breeze in here!" said Bernadette's mother. "Please close that fridge, unless you're trying to trap a polar bear."

"But I need to make my own lunch for tomorrow."

"What do you want?"

"Brown food."

"Since when do you organize your food by color?"

"Since I joined the Lunch Bunch today," Bernadette declared.

"And what, pray tell, is the Lunch Bunch?" asked her mother, laughing.

"A strategy for surviving the lunchroom!"

"Well, I'm all for *that*! So a brown lunch it is."

Bernadette's mother rummaged around a little and came up with the following menu: lentil soup, whole wheat bread, a box of raisins, and some chocolate chip cookies

"Soup is good," said Bernadette. "Annie always brings soup. And can you toast the bread and cut it in little strips instead of big triangles? That's how Megan always eats her bread. And may I please have fifty cents for chocolate milk? Keisha always buys chocolate milk."

"Is Annie Wang part of the Lunch Bunch?"

"Yup."

"Can I assume that Megan and Keisha, who I've never heard of before, are also in this mysterious Lunch Bunch?"

"Yup."

"I told you you'd make new friends if you ate lunch at school."

"Yes, I know. I should always listen to my mother."

"Absolutely. Mother knows best. And now I need to know what this strategy is going to do to my grocery shopping. Do your meals have to be a different color every single day?"

"No, no. That's just *one* strategy. I'm busy thinking of others."

"Thinking of strategies is definitely your kind of thing, Bernadette. The girls in the Lunch Bunch are going to be very happy you joined them!"

And they were. First of all, Bernadette persuaded the others that they should save their special strategies for Fridays so they would have something to look forward to all week. The first Friday was a Make-Your-Own-Sandwich Day. The girls brought bread and crackers, and different kinds of toppings to share. Annie brought salmon salad and sliced hard-boiled eggs; Megan brought turkey and cherry tomatoes and a tiny pot of mayonnaise; Keisha brought cream cheese and homemade strawberry jam, and Bernadette brought salsa and grated cheese and lettuce and a few slices of avocado that turned into disgusting brown mush and had to be thrown out.

The second Friday was a dinner party, so they each had to bring a place mat and a cloth napkin and forks and spoons to eat with. Annie brought tiny blue and white china tea cups that they poured their juice into, Keisha brought some beautiful napkin rings shaped like tropical birds,

Megan brought a single rose in a little vase, and Bernadette made place cards with an after-dinner mint stuck on each one with tape. The kids at the noisy table made fun of them, but Bernadette didn't care.

The third Friday was a picnic. They got permission to eat in the schoolyard with Ms. Chin,

the librarian, who always ate her own lunch outside under the willow tree when the weather was
nice. After lunch they helped her in the library,
filing books and tidying the shelves. And because
they were such good helpers, Ms. Chin said they
could help in the library any time they wanted.
Helping in the library was fun, and they always
got to take out the new books before anybody
else, when the pages still smelled like ink, and the
spines crackled with knowledge, and the covers
were shiny and bright. And by then, Bernadette
hardly ever wished she could go home for lunch
anymore.

5

The Best Birthday Ever!

Coming up with strategies for school lunches was easy for Bernadette because one of her favorite things to do was experiment in the kitchen. "A kitchen is just like a laboratory," she declared. "After all, in a kitchen, you heat stuff up or cool it down just like you do in a lab. In a kitchen, you make lots of disgusting smells, just like you do in a lab. And in a kitchen, you measure all kinds of strange ingredients and mix them together to get something that nobody in the world has ever made before. But the *best* part of working in a kitchen is that you get to eat all your experiments!"

When she was really little, she used to make simple things like corn flakes topped with peas and carrots, because she wasn't allowed to use the stove or to cut things up with knives. But once Jasmine started coming over they created what they called "magical mystery meals." These were complicated dishes like tomatoes stuffed with vanilla ice cream, or baked potatoes covered with peanut butter and jam. Their most famous invention was probably the chocolate-chip pepperoni cookie, which only Bernadette's father had been brave enough to try. "Yummy!" he said, "but I don't want to spoil my appetite for supper, so one bite is enough for me."

Because she enjoyed cooking so much, Bernadette also loved parties. Having a party was even better than making a meal because parties involved extra planning. You had to decide not only what to eat but also who to invite, how to decorate the room, and which games to play. Unfortunately, her parents were not interested in her advice when it came to their own parties, but they always let her plan her very own once-a-year birthday celebrations.

Bernadette's first successful event was her sixth birthday party. Even though it was starting to get cold out, she decided on a beach theme. Her parents emptied the playroom and put a big sheet of plastic over the tile floor. Then they filled up her wading pool with nice warm water, and Bernadette and two cousins and Marcus from next door and her best friend Jasmine splashed away happily in their bathing suits. After they dried off, they drank pineapple juice in tall glasses filled with ice cubes and cherries, with little paper umbrellas sticking out the top. They ate hot dogs and potato chips and ice cream cones, and made sand paintings, and everyone got a new pair of sunglasses to take home. Everyone agreed that the beach party was brilliant, and so was Bernadette.

When she turned seven she had a zoo party. All her guests brought their favorite stuffed animals and made a puppet show with them. They played Animal Snap and Pin the Tail on the Donkey and Duck Duck Goose and then went fishing for little plastic animals in a big bowl. Unfortunately, Marcus and her little cousin Brian wanted the same toy, and they started fighting over it. To break up the fight, Bernadette's mother made everyone listen to the story of "How the Elephant Got His Nose." Bernadette was mad at her mother for interrupting the fishing game and refused to laugh even when the Elephant's Child spanked all his dear families. And she kept on sulking while everyone else made cookies using her brand new animal-shaped cookie cutters, and baked them, and decorated them with four colors of icing and three kinds of sprinkles. She only cheered up when

Jasmine made her an extra special elephant cookie with pink and purple stripes and told her she was her best friend in the whole entire world.

Bernadette had started thinking about what to do for her eighth birthday the day she turned seven. Then Jasmine moved away, and she stopped thinking about it, because how could her birthday party be any fun without Jasmine? But now she was friends with the girls in the Lunch Bunch, and even though she still had a lonely place in her heart when she thought about Jasmine, she was determined to have the best birthday party ever!

The problem was that she had so *many* ideas, she couldn't make up her mind. Should each of her guests come dressed as a character from a book, or should they go bowling instead? Should they draw pictures on T-shirts or do scientific experiments? Did she want to have a supper party and serve real food like spaghetti and meatballs, or would it be better to have a tea party with lots and lots of good snacks? Two weeks before Bernadette's birthday, her father took her to the library to do some research. They took out a huge stack of books full of party ideas and Bernadette looked through them to find something, *anything,* to do for her birthday. Meanwhile her father sat in a big comfy chair with his eyes closed, listening to music on his iPod.

"I give up, Daddy," she finally declared. "Let's go home."

"What did you say, Honey? Did you find something you like?"

"NO! I DID NOT FIND ANYTHING I LIKED!" Bernadette shouted so loudly that the librarian came running to see what was the matter. Her father apologized, and rushed her out of the library and into the car.

They sat in silence all the way home. Bernadette couldn't think of a single thing she really wanted to do on her birthday. She slammed the car door and stomped up the steps of her house, without saying "thank you" to her father or "hello" to her mother.

"Arg," said her mother. "Why are you so fierce?"

"That's *it*!" cried Bernadette. "What a great idea! Thanks, Mom."

"What great idea?"

"Your idea for my birthday party. We'll dress up as pirates, and go around saying 'Arg' and 'Yo Ho Ho,' and 'Avast, me hearties!!' We can have sword fights, and a treasure hunt, and walk the plank, and sleep over on a desert island."

"No sword fighting, sorry. It frightens the natives. But other than that, a pirate party is a super idea," said her mom, relieved that Bernadette had finally decided what to do.

When the Lunch Bunch showed up for the Best Birthday Ever, they looked amazing. Annie had a patch over one eye and a big gold earring in one ear; she wore a long white shirt of her mother's, belted at the waist with a pretend sword sticking out. Megan had black rubber boots and a red and white striped shirt and a triangle hat with a red feather in it. She came into the house clutching a plastic knife between her teeth. Keisha wore a polka dot kerchief over her hair and a toy parrot stuck to her shoulder. She had a vest covered with gold spangles and bright purple satin pants. Bernadette herself wore a golden cape and a blackened front tooth and a curly black moustache that kept making her sneeze. Best of all, she had a hook covering one hand. It was really made of aluminum foil wrapped around a Styrofoam cup but it looked very convincing, except to Hamlet the guinea pig, who took a little nibble just to see if aluminum foil was tasty.

The first activity was to follow a treasure map all around the house looking for the shiny plastic rings and candy necklaces and chocolate coins Bernadette's mother had hidden in the laundry basket, under the sofa, and behind the TV. Then the girls ate a chocolate cake shaped like a treasure chest covered with gold coins, and drank cranberry

juice from real wine glasses. Finally they each were given a little wooden box to decorate with pearls and sequins and paint and stickers. But Megan didn't use stickers or anything else to cover her box. Instead, she painted a beautiful mermaid across its lid, a squiggly pink octopus on one side, and a lot of tiny orange and yellow fish darting through dark green seaweed on the others. She painted the whole background a watery blue.

The other girls stuck so much glittery stuff all over their treasure chests that they used up all the glue, and Bernadette's father had to make an emergency run to the store to buy some more. But that was OK, because Megan was painting so slowly and carefully, drawing little curves for each shiny scale of the mermaid's tail, that she still wasn't finished when he came back.

"Wow, Megan, you are a *wonderful* artist!" said Bernadette's mother.

"I told you, Mom, didn't I?" said Bernadette,

proudly. Everyone in the Lunch Bunch seemed spectacularly talented to her.

"You're an artist too, aren't you, Mrs. Schwartz?" asked Megan.

"Yes, I am. Is that what you want to do when you grow up?"

"I think so. It would be nice to have a job that makes you happy. My father has to travel all the time for his job and it makes him so tired and grumpy. And he never gets to have fun with us; even on the weekend, he still keeps working."

"My mother loves her job," Keisha said. "She says it gives her life meaning."

"What does she do?" asked Bernadette's mother.

"She's a nurse," said Keisha proudly.

"It takes a special person to be a nurse. You have to be very smart, and also very kind and patient."

"My mom is almost like a nurse," said Annie.

"What does she do?" asked Bernadette's father.

"She and my dad are both optometrists. They have their own store downtown where they make eyeglasses for people."

"You should go see them, Daddy," said Bernadette. "Maybe they could make you some super special glasses that would stay on your head with magnets so that you could never lose them!"

"Ha, ha. Very funny, Bernadette," said her father.

"My mom only works at the store three days a week now, because my grandpa's sick, and it's too hard for Grandma to take care of him and my baby brother at the same time," Annie said.

"Annie has so many people in her house," said Bernadette. "She has her parents, and three brothers, and both her grandparents."

"Don't forget my auntie who lives in the

downstairs apartment," said Annie. "Sometimes she comes upstairs to eat supper with us. And sometimes her boyfriend comes too."

"It must get pretty noisy over there," said Bernadette's father.

"My big brother walks around with headphones on all the time so he doesn't have to hear us," Annie laughed.

"You do that to me too, Daddy, and I'm just one little tiny girl," said Bernadette.

"A little tiny girl who never stops talking!" said Bernadette's father. "Bernadette even talks in her sleep, girls. You'll find out tonight."

All the girls were planning to sleep over—even Megan, who usually didn't feel comfortable away from home, and had to call her mother to say goodnight, and even cried a tiny little bit until Annie gave her a big hug and said, "You have to stay, Megan! Without you it won't be any fun. You are not only an amazing artist, you are a very important member of the Lunch Bunch. And tomorrow we will become the Breakfast Bunch, so we need you."

"My mom said we could make pancakes," said Bernadette. "And I have some secret ingredients picked out to make them extra special."

"Like crayons and mustard," said Keisha. "Yum!"

"Or guinea pig kibble and shampoo," said Annie. "Double yum!"

"Don't be so silly, you guys!" said Bernadette. "If you keep saying stuff like that, you'll scare Megan away for sure."

But by this time Megan wasn't crying anymore. She was laughing so hard that she decided to stay.

It took the girls a while to set up the playroom exactly the way they wanted it. First they used sheets and chairs and pillows to make a tent, so they could pretend they were stranded on a desert island. Everything kept falling down, but finally there was enough space inside for all four of them to unroll their sleeping bags. When the tent was ready, they changed into their pajamas, and Bernadette's father made them hot chocolate with little marshmallows floating in it and slices of apple sprinkled with cinnamon and sugar.

"I don't think *real* pirates drink hot chocolate, Daddy," said Bernadette.

"I don't think *real* pirates wear pink nightgowns either," her father replied, winking at Annie. She was also wearing bunny slippers, and didn't look very frightening anymore.

"Maybe the lady pirates do!" said Annie. "Besides, all my other pajamas were in the wash."

"Real pirates never wash their clothes," said Keisha.

"Yuck!" said Megan. "I'm glad we're not real pirates then."

"Since you aren't real pirates, you have permission to brush your teeth," Bernadette's mother said, laughing. "Now scoot, it's getting late. And I don't want you girls to stay up all night talking."

"My mother says they should be called '*wake-overs*,' not 'sleepovers', because nobody ever gets to sleep," Keisha said.

"I'll come and check on you landlubbers in half an hour, and whoever is still up will have to walk the plank!" said Bernadette's father, in a very growly voice.

"Give us more than half an hour, Daddy, it's a special BIRTHDAY sleepover," begged Bernadette.

"Give us an hour please, Mr. Bernadette's Dad," said Keisha.

"Forty-five minutes and not one minute more," Bernadette's father declared.

But when he came downstairs forty-five minutes later, everyone was quiet, even Bernadette, and fast asleep, even Megan. And they all slept until late the next morning, when they made pancakes with bananas, and raspberries, and chocolate chips, and whipped cream. And although Bernadette had hoped to try some more unusual ingredients, she had to agree that the Lunch Bunch made the best birthday pancakes ever.

6

The Talent Show

Jasmine's moving away was the absolutely worst thing that happened to Bernadette in Grade Three, although not being allowed in the science fair was almost as bad. And there were a lot of other not-very-good things, like getting the strictest teacher in the school and sitting next to Jackie Renfrew in class. Having to eat lunch at school every day started out terribly, although that turned out OK because of the Lunch Bunch. But just when she thought all the terrible things that could happen to her had already happened, Bernadette found out about the talent show.

One day, with no warning at all, the principal made an announcement. "*Bonjour, mes enfants*," she said. "I have some very exciting news. This year, for the very first time, we will be having a talent show. The First Annual Garden Road Elementary School Talent Show will be taking place three weeks from today! And I just can't wait to see what all you wonderful kids can do."

Jackie Renfrew immediately started jumping up and down with excitement.

"Imitating a yo-yo is *not* a talent, Jackie," said Mrs. Hawthorn.

"Is doing gymnastics a talent, Mrs. Hawthorn?" asked Annie.

"Certainly."

"What about playing the recorder?" asked Megan.

"Of course."

"Can I sing a funny song from camp?" asked Keisha.

"That's an excellent idea," said Mrs. Hawthorn. "But as the principal said, you have three weeks to plan for the talent show, so now it's time to settle down, even though I understand that you're all excited."

But Bernadette was *not* excited. She did not join discussions about which was harder to play, the piano or the violin, or which was more fun, ballet or jazz dance, or which was more dangerous, karate or judo. She had no opinion, because she didn't do any of these activities. The only classes she took outside of school were swimming lessons, because Canada has three oceans and the most fresh water of any country on the planet, and Bernadette thought it was very important to know how to swim. But apart from swimming, Bernadette Inez O'Brian Schwartz was always so busy with her various projects, hobbies, and experiments that she didn't have time to develop any talent-show kinds of talents.

It was obvious to her teacher that *something* was wrong, because Bernadette had not asked a single question all afternoon.

"What's bothering you, Bernadette?" Mrs. Hawthorn asked her at the end of the day.

"I just realized something truly, completely, *horrible*," Bernadette moaned.

"Did you forget to study for the spelling test?" asked her teacher.

"No," said Bernadette. "This is something much worse, Mrs. Hawthorn. I just realized that I don't have any talents."

"That's not true, Bernadette, everybody has talents," said Mrs. Hawthorn.

"Name one of mine!" said Bernadette.

"Well for starters, you're a wizard at science."

"Which is exactly why I need to be in the SCIENCE FAIR, Mrs. Hawthorn. Why can't I be in the science fair instead of the stupid talent show? Science is my real talent; you just said so yourself."

"But you don't have to be in the talent show at all if you don't want to," said Mrs. Hawthorn. "After all, it's supposed to be fun."

"What fun will it be to just sit and watch everybody else?" said Bernadette, in a very grumpy voice. "Annie's going to do gymnastics, and Megan is going to play the recorder, and Keisha is going to sing that song from her summer camp even though everyone is sick of hearing it already. And we always do everything together because we're the Lunch Bunch, but I can't, because I don't have any talents."

"They will still be your friends even if you're not in the talent show, Bernadette. After all, *somebody* has to be in the audience! Now go line up at the door with the rest of the class, please. School is over for today."

Bernadette dragged her feet all the way home, trying to figure out if she had any secret hidden talents she had somehow forgotten about. But she couldn't think of anything, unless she counted skipping on one foot, or counting backwards from one hundred by twos, or pulling out her own loose tooth, or remembering to feed her guinea pig, without being reminded more than twice. She was very proud that she had passed the deep end test at the pool, but there was no way she could swim in the gym.

Her mother, who she could usually rely on for good ideas, was no help at all.

"Why don't you and Keisha put on a puppet show?" her mother suggested. "You always make up such great stories when she comes over to play. You could take our puppet theater to school for the day."

"Putting on a puppet show is not a talent," said Bernadette.

"Who says?" objected her mother.

"Everyone!" Bernadette replied. "A talent is something you do with your own body, like ballet, or singing, or riding a skateboard. And I can't do any of those things."

"I think you have a lovely voice, dear," Bernadette's mother said loyally.

"Oh yeah? Then how come Mr. Big-Ears Lepage sticks me in the back row in music class, and keeps asking me to sing more softly?"

"Oh my! You never told me about that. Then maybe singing isn't such a good idea after all. But you can dance, can't you?"

"No, I can't. I *hate* dancing. It's too floppy, and when it's not floppy it's jerky, and whatever you're doing makes you look like a sick chicken."

"Maybe Uncle Rob could teach you some magic tricks. He was really good at them when he was a boy. He used to perform at all my birthday parties, and my friends thought he was terrific."

"Magic tricks are boring. Everybody always figures them out right away."

"Well, as long as you have such a bad attitude, Bernadette, I don't see how I can help you!"

"Nobody can help me!" wailed Bernadette. "That's exactly the problem. Why didn't you and Daddy send me to piano lessons or something? Now I'm the only girl in Grade Three with NO TALENTS!"

"Sweetie, talent is not something you learn. Talent is something you *have*. And you have so many talents! You're the smartest kid I know," said her mother, giving her a huge hug.

"So what!" said Bernadette, struggling out of the hug. "You can't show people 'being smart.' What should I do? Just stand there and *think*?" And with that, she burst out crying, ran into her bedroom, and slammed the door.

One week passed, then two, and finally three. The Lunch Bunch was ruined because no matter how good a strategy Bernadette came up with—even getting a *pizza* delivered to their table in the lunchroom—all Megan and Annie and Keisha could talk about was the stupid talent show! But the more excited the other girls got, the more left out Bernadette felt. If it had just been a Grade Three talent show, she might have been willing to learn some magic tricks from Uncle Rob. If it had just been a Grade Three talent show, she might have been willing to do a stupid chicken dance. But the whole of Garden Road Elementary School would be sitting there watching, and the whole of Garden Road Elementary School would make fun of her if she made a mistake. And Bernadette Inez O'Brian Schwartz hated making mistakes more than she hated anything else.

She hated making mistakes more than she hated getting no cherries in her fruit cocktail.

She hated making mistakes more than she hated putting on a wet bathing suit. She hated making mistakes more than she hated going to bed when it was still light out in the summer. She really REALLY, **REALLY** hated making mistakes—especially in front of other people!

On the day of the talent show, it seemed like everyone in Bernadette's class was happy except Bernadette.

"Aren't you in the talent show, Bernadette?" asked Jackie Renfrew, who was turning out to be not only the most annoying boy in class, but also the most annoying boy in the whole entire universe and beyond.

"No," said Bernadette.

"Why not? All your friends are in it."

"You don't have to remind me," said Bernadette, deciding that she would **never, ever** help Jackie with a math problem again.

"Are you shy?" Jackie asked, in a very quiet voice. Bernadette was so surprised she looked straight at him. He had green eyes just like a cat, and freckles in a straight line across his nose.

"No. Are you?"

"I used to hate people looking at me. I was sure they were thinking I was puny, or stupid, or something," Jackie said.

Bernadette felt guilty, since these were all things she had thought about Jackie at one time or another.

"How did you stop feeling shy?"

"I found out I was really good at violin. When I'm playing the violin, I just forget that other people are there, so I don't mind them watching me anymore."

"That must be nice," sighed Bernadette. "I'm not good at anything."

"What are you talking about?" said Jackie. "You're good at lots of things! I'm only good at violin."

"Well, today I wish I could play the violin like you," said Bernadette, "because then I could be in the talent show."

"My grandpa always says everybody is good at something, but nobody can be good at *everything*."

Then they stopped talking, because Mrs. Hawthorn made them line up by twos and go down quietly to the gym for the talent show. But it didn't matter, because all of a sudden Bernadette felt better than she had for three whole weeks. A bright blue bubble of happiness floated up from her stomach, lifting her spirits with it. She *was* good at lots of things, even if they weren't the kind of things she could show off at a talent show.

And because she was feeling better, she was able to enjoy Annie's back walkover and Keisha's silly song. Because she was feeling better, she could see that Jackie Renfrew really was

AMAZING on the violin. He was so amazing that all the teachers stood up to cheer for him and yelled, "Encore!" And because she was feeling better, she noticed something else that made her think that next year she *could* be in the talent show if she still wanted to.

She noticed that almost everybody—except Jackie Renfrew—made mistakes! The Kindergarten girls messed up their ballet, but nobody cared because, after all, they were only in Kindergarten. The tall Grade Six boy who was juggling six oranges dropped one, but no one cared because, after all, juggling six oranges is very hard. Even her friend Megan forgot the notes on her recorder and had to start over from the beginning, but she played "Greensleeves" so perfectly the second time that everybody applauded. Then, when she sat down next to Bernadette with a red face and eyes full of tears and said, "I blew it," Bernadette replied, "Of course you blew it! You *have* to blow it. That's how a recorder works, silly," and they both started laughing.

Then Mrs. Hawthorn hissed, "Bernadette Inez O'BRIAN **SCHWARTZ**! Be quiet *this instant*!" And Jackie Renfrew, who was sitting on Bernadette's other side, leaned over and whispered, "I know what your talent is, Bernadette! Your talent is having four names that everybody always remembers!"

7

Making Megan Smile

Because her mother's job was illustrating books, every room in Bernadette's house had a bookcase in it. To eat a meal at the kitchen table, you had to clear away layers of newspapers and magazines. Her father was always losing his glasses under one pile or another, and sometimes Bernadette's homework disappeared if she wasn't careful where she put it. Once, when he was taking his evening stroll around the living room, Hamlet the guinea pig chewed up the corner of Bernadette's report card.

Eating paper was one of Hamlet's favorite hobbies, so Bernadette's house was a very good home for him.

Despite having a house full of books, Bernadette's mother still liked to go to the public library, and Bernadette liked to go there too. The children's section had a cozy sofa covered in red velvet, and extra small tables and chairs, and books on low shelves for little hands to reach. There was also a fireplace that didn't work, but was big enough to curl up inside if you got there before anyone else did. Sometimes people fought over the fireplace until the librarian came running over and said, "*SHHHHHH*," in a very cross voice. Bernadette had noticed that when librarians told people to be quiet, they were usually a lot noisier than the people they were complaining about. But she didn't think it would be a very good idea to point this out to them.

Over the fireplace stood a row of dolls and stuffed animals representing famous characters like Anne of Green Gables and Harry Potter and the Wild Things from *Where the Wild Things Are*. The babies who came to the library were allowed to play with these toys while the toddlers had story time and the big kids did their homework or played games on the computers. Bernadette liked sitting on the floor with the babies. While they chewed on the Anne doll's red pigtails and drooled all over the Wild Things, she looked at picture books with illustrations of talking animals and beautiful princesses or browsed though the easy readers to see if there were any good ones she'd missed. Then she would read them very fast, trying to break her own record of Most Books Read in a Single Week. So far the best she'd done was twelve, but she figured that was pretty good for a girl who was only eight years old and practically the shortest person in her class.

What Bernadette loved best of all was to take home chapter books, now that she was old enough to read them herself. Sometimes her mother and father still read to her at bedtime anyway, because her whole family loved hearing stories out loud. Ms. Chin, the librarian at Garden Road Elementary School, also liked to read out loud. She was an amazing actress and could do a lot of different voices. If you closed your eyes, you would think that at least four or five people were talking and not just one pretty lady sitting in a rocking chair reading from a book.

"When you read by yourself, do you still do all those different voices?" Bernadette asked her one day.

"Sort of," said Ms. Chin. "I hear them talking inside me. But I don't do them out loud! It would be kind of embarrassing reading out loud on a bus, or sitting in a coffee shop, don't you think?"

"I saw a man walking down the street last week

talking to himself," said Annie. "He was waving his arms around too. My mother said not to stare because he was probably crazy or drunk, but I didn't think he looked crazy or drunk. I'll bet he was a movie star, practicing his part."

"I want to be a movie star when I grow up," said Keisha. "You have to practice a lot to learn your lines by heart."

"Being an actor is a wonderful job," said Ms. Chin, "And reading books is great practice for being an actor because when you read a book, you get to play *all* the parts, not just one."

"A girl can have a boy's adventure and a boy can be a girl," added Megan.

"I like imagining that I'm a famous person like Madame Curie," Annie said.

"I prefer being a dump-truck," said Bernadette. "Or an ice-cream sundae. With extra sprinkles."

"This is getting silly, girls," said Ms. Chin, laughing. "Let's get back to work."

They were supposed to be putting books on the shelves at the Garden Road Elementary School Library. Sometimes after lunch, Bernadette and her friends helped Ms. Chin take all the books that had been returned by students that week and put them back where they belonged according to the Dewey Decimal System. Although not as vast as the Solar System or as important as the Digestive System, Bernadette thought the Dewey Decimal System was a pretty good way to organize things—just not quite as good as her own system. At home, Bernadette organized her storybooks by the authors' last names, and her reference books by subject. On her own personal bookshelf, "birds" came before "bugs" and "guinea pigs" came after "fish." But at school things were more complicated. You couldn't just look up "animals." You had to look up the kind of animal you were interested in, and you had to know things like whether it lived on a farm or was wild in nature, and whether it was extinct like a dinosaur or alive like a puppy. It could be frustrating, because to find a book on a subject, you already had to know something about the subject!

Still, Bernadette liked filing books, because in the library, things were where they were supposed to be. Sometimes in real life, they moved around. For example, the week after Bernadette's birthday, Megan's dad had moved out of the house, leaving Megan and her little brother, Connor, alone with their mother. They were probably going to get divorced. Of course Bernadette had heard of divorce; her Uncle Rob had been divorced before he married Auntie Beth. But her mother said that didn't really count because he got married too young the first time, and anyway, since he and his first wife didn't have kids, they weren't hurting anybody's feelings but their own. Unfortunately, Megan's feelings were hurt a lot, and there was nothing The Lunch Bunch could do to make her feel better.

Also, because Megan was going to be staying at her father's new apartment on the other side of town every second weekend, it would make it harder for the other girls to spend time with her. She told them that her father had bought her and Connor bunk beds and matching desks, and let them pick out the wallpaper for their new room. He even got them a hamster named Mr. McWhiskers. Things weren't all bad. Still, wasn't a family supposed to stay the same? Bernadette didn't like it when things didn't stay in the proper categories.

Even Megan wasn't where she was supposed to be. She kept missing school. Some days she didn't come at all; other days she arrived late. A few times she showed up in the morning, but later said she had a stomachache and wanted to go home. Mrs. Hawthorn sent her to the office, and the secretary called her mother to come get her. Usually her mother would rush right over and they'd zoom off like it was a real emergency. But once, when her mother was too busy to come, the principal just gave Megan a glass of water with a blue-and-white-striped straw in it, and let her sit on the sofa in her office until she felt better.

The third time Megan went home was the day of Jackie Renfrew's birthday. Jackie's mother and father brought him to school that morning with a beautiful cake shaped like a violin, and paper plates and napkins, and a plastic container full of ripe strawberries. Mrs. Hawthorn said they could have a party in the classroom after recess. All the kids were excited except for Megan. She said her stomach hurt too much for her to eat anything, even birthday cake, and then she went home.

"But Megan *loves* birthday cake," Bernadette said to the other girls after Megan went home. "She ate more at my party than anybody else did!"

"I know," said Annie.

"Why do you think she keeps going home?" asked Keisha.

"Maybe she's afraid that her mom will move out just like her father did," said Bernadette slowly. "So she wants to keep an eye on her."

"Do you really think so?" said Keisha. "That seems a little weird. Where would her mother go?"

"I don't know," Annie replied. "But I agree with Bernadette. Imagine if *your* dad moved out of *your* house. You might start to act a little weird too."

"Maybe Megan's stomach really does hurt, from being worried. My mom gets headaches when she's stressed out at the hospital," Keisha said.

"My auntie gets migraines sometimes," said Annie. "She has to stay in bed with the curtains closed so that the light doesn't bother her eyes."

"Megan's not having migraines," said

Bernadette. "She's just sad, that's all. She's too sad to concentrate on school, and she's too sad to have fun with us."

"So we have an important mission," said Annie. "It's our job to cheer her up."

"This mission needs a code name," said Keisha.

"What about 'Making Megan Smile'?" asked Bernadette.

"I like it!" said Annie.

"Me too," said Keisha. "But there's only one problem. How do we do it?"

"This mission should have something to do with art, I think," Bernadette said. "Because making art is Megan's favorite thing. And it's hard for people to be sad when they're doing their favorite thing."

"Maybe we could buy her some new art supplies?" Annie suggested. "I saw an ad for markers that smell like fruit. Those would be cool."

"Maybe," said Keisha, doubtfully. "But Megan has tons of art supplies already. And even though she might be happy to get some new stuff, I don't think that would make her want to come to school."

"But having more art at school would make her want to come!" said Bernadette. "I never want to skip school anymore because I like the science experiments we do in Mrs. Hawthorn's class. So we need to find a way to do more art, and then Megan will start enjoying school again."

"Not just more art, Bernadette," Keisha said. "*Better* art. I know that Megan is tired of making masks out of paper plates and feathers, or gluing tissue paper onto pickle jars to make pretty vases. We need to get some kind of fantastic project that will make her want to be here every single day!"

"All the fantastic projects are for big kids," Bernadette said. "Like the school musical. Or the hockey tournament. Or the SCIENCE FAIR!"

"So we need to find something new. Something that's never been done before." said Annie.

"A fantastic, new, art project. A fantastic, new art project that the Grade Threes are allowed to do," said Keisha. "What could that possibly be?"

"We're the Lunch Bunch, guys," said Bernadette. "We specialize in thinking of strategies. So we should be able to think of something that will make Megan smile!"

They thought as hard as they could all day, but they couldn't agree on a good idea. When Bernadette's mother picked her up, she could tell right away that something was wrong. Annie, Keisha, and Bernadette were sitting together looking very gloomy and silent under the weeping willow tree.

"What's the matter?" she asked. "Usually after school you guys have wall-to-wall smiles."

"That's *it*!" cried Bernadette. "What a great idea! Thanks, Mom."

"What great idea?"

"You just gave me an idea for our mission. We'll get Megan to do a giant painting on a wall."

"That's called a mural," said her mother.

"No, it's called 'Making Megan Smile'," said Keisha, laughing.

"Now we just have to get Mrs. Garcia to agree, and figure out *which* wall needs painting," Bernadette added. "This old building is looking pretty run down, don't you think? How can anyone expect to keep children happy and productive in such a gloomy environment?"

"Now let me get this straight," said Bernadette's mother. "You want to ask the principal to let Megan paint a mural somewhere in your school?"

"Exactly! And you need to come with us when we ask her, since it really was your idea. Besides, since you are an artist yourself, you can tell Mrs. Garcia what supplies she needs to buy."

"I see my grandma coming," said Annie. "Just let me tell her to wait for me while we talk to the principal."

"And I'll go tell my big sister," said Keisha.

"Mrs. Garcia," said Bernadette, when they all got to the principal's office, "We have an idea for you."

"By 'we,' do you mean you and your mother, or you and your friends?" asked the principal, laughing.

"All of us. My mom is here to help, because it's an *art* idea, and she's an artist."

"OK, fire away," said Mrs. Garcia. "I always like art ideas!"

"Well, people like to come to school when they get to do their favorite thing. Like me, for instance. My favorite thing is science, so I've been planning to be in the science fair since Grade One. But now I can't be in it because the school board changed the rules, which you have to admit isn't fair."

"Bernadette," said Keisha, "Our mission is to cheer up Megan, not to complain about the science fair."

"This is about Megan?" said the principal.

"Yes," explained Annie. "You know how she's always getting sick these days? Well, we thought that maybe if she had a special art project to do, Megan would stop feeling sick and she would want to stay at school. Because she loves art."

"And we thought a good project would be making a giant painting on a wall, which, in case you didn't know, is called a mural," added Bernadette.

"I think that's a brilliant idea, girls. Megan is lucky to have such good friends! And I know exactly the right place for a mural. We just tore down a set of bookshelves to make more space in the music room, so that wall needs to be painted anyway."

"So when can she start?" asked Bernadette.

"Well, wait a minute," said Mrs. Garcia. "Let's not rush into things without thinking this through properly. Do you girls want Megan to know that we made up this project just for her?"

"No way!" said Keisha, "I know Megan really well, and she would hate thinking that everybody feels sorry for her."

"Mrs. Garcia, why can't you make the mural a project for *all* the Grade Threes?" suggested Bernadette. "Since Megan is by far the best artist in Grade Three, she will automatically end up being one of the kids who does it."

"That's a very clever strategy, Bernadette," said Mrs. Garcia.

"Bernadette specializes in strategies," said Annie.

"And I specialize in supporting them," said

Bernadette's mother. "So I'd be happy to help buy materials, or supervise the design, if that would be useful."

"What a team!" said Mrs. Garcia. "I think this is a great plan, and it might actually work. Let's give it a shot."

The very next day Mrs. Garcia announced that there was going to be an art project just for the Grade Three students at Garden Road Elementary School: a mural for the back wall of the music room! Both Grade Three classes were going to get a half hour every day for the next week to work on their designs. Then a real professional artist was going to come in and help the music teacher and the principal choose the very best design, and the artist who made it would be in charge of a team of painters to work at lunchtime, and after school, until the mural was done.

Megan listened to the announcement and

she began to smile. The smile started in her eyes, which sparkled for the first time in a long time. Then the corners of her mouth turned up in little happy commas. And then she started to grin. She was remembering how much everyone had loved the box she had painted at Bernadette's party.

"When can we start, Mrs. Hawthorn?" she asked.

"Now would be a very good time, I think," her teacher answered.

"I am *so* glad I came to school today!" exclaimed Megan.

Bernadette wrote, "Mission accomplished" on a piece of paper, and passed it to Annie. And even though Mrs. Hawthorn hated students passing notes in class, she didn't say anything. She just winked, and handed out paper and colored pencils.

8

Bernadette's Experiment

It was the second Friday in December, and the tenth time the Lunch Bunch had to come up with a strategy. This week, the strategy was alphabetical. Each girl could only eat food beginning with same letter as her name.

"What did you bring, Megan? asked Bernadette.

"Macaroni, mixed salad, a muffin, and two mandarin oranges," Megan said. "I'm pretty happy. This is one of the best lunches I've ever had!"

"Mine is better!" said Keisha, opening her lunchbox to show them a kebab on a kaiser roll with ketchup, a kiwi, and a Kit-Kat bar. "'K' was such a hard letter, my mother let me have a chocolate bar for desert. Yippee!"

"You're lucky," said Annie. "My grandpa had to go to the hospital yesterday, so we didn't have time to go grocery shopping. All I could find at home that started with the letter 'A' was alphabet soup and an apple."

"You can have half my Kit-Kat if you want," said Keisha.

"And half my buttered bagel," said Bernadette. "Is your Grandpa going to be OK, Annie?"

"I hope so, because we were planning to go skiing over Christmas vacation, but my mom won't want to go away if he's still in the hospital. What else do you have for lunch, Bernadette?"

"Blueberry yogurt, a banana, and bean salad. I hate bean salad, so you can have that too if you want it."

"'Buttered bagel' makes a good tongue twister," said Keisha. "Try saying it five times quickly."

"It five times quickly!" said Bernadette.

"I *knew* you were going to say that, Bernadette," groaned Keisha.

"Well, why do you keep turning everything we say into tongue twisters?"

"It's good practice," said Keisha. "We always do tongue twisters as warm-ups before every rehearsal."

Keisha had a lead role in the Christmas pageant at her church, so she had to go to a lot of rehearsals. All the girls in the Lunch Bunch were looking forward to seeing her perform, but meanwhile she had no time to play with them after school or on weekends because she was so busy. Megan was very busy too, working away on her mural for the music room during lunch hour every day, and sometimes after school as well. Everyone had agreed that her design of cats, dogs, and birds playing musical instruments was amazing, but because it was so complicated it was taking a very long time to finish.

Of course, this was a good thing, because it kept Megan from skipping school, which had been the point of the mural in the first place. But even though Megan was happy again, Bernadette was starting to feel a little left out. The other girls in the Lunch Bunch were so excited about their own special activities—even Annie, who was getting ready for her big ski trip, and had been shopping every weekend for new clothes and equipment— that none of them cared about the science fair coming up next week.

All the older kids at Garden Road Elementary School were full of excitement. Annie's big brother was turning a potato into a transistor radio. Keisha's big sister was making natural pigments from fruits and vegetables, and her cousin was making a funny-looking machine with two eggbeaters and a lot of wires to do something he refused to explain. "Visit the science fair and see!" he said, when Bernadette asked what it was going to be.

But Bernadette didn't want to visit the science fair if she couldn't be in it! Not being in the talent show had made her feel bad because the rest of the Lunch Bunch had the right kind of talents and she didn't. But not being in the science fair was a thousand times worse, because science WAS her very own special talent! She tried to explain this to her friends, but even though they felt sorry for her, none of them cared about science the way she did.

"The only person who really understands me is Jasmine," Bernadette moaned to her mother. "But she's never around when I need her most!"

"Well, the holidays are almost here and then Jasmine will be coming for a visit," said her mother. "Aren't you excited about that?"

"Yes, but it's only a *visit,* Mom. Then she'll go away again. And I miss her more now than I did at the beginning of the year, because nobody cares about the science fair but me! I thought that Mrs. Hawthorn would understand how I feel, but she keeps changing the subject whenever I bring it up. So I've decided that I don't like her after all, and I don't think we should give her a Christmas present."

"Come on Bernadette, it's not your *teacher's* fault that the school board changed its rules. And you have to admit that you are learning a lot of science in Mrs. Hawthorn's class. What about that research project the Lunch Bunch did on the life cycle of a butterfly? That was fantastic!"

"Yeah, I guess it was pretty good," said Bernadette, grudgingly. "Especially with Megan's drawings."

"See? You don't need to be in a science fair to do science, Bernadette, and you know it. Real scientists learn things every day, not just on special occasions," said her mother. "So is it OK if I give Mrs. Hawthorn the present we bought her?"

"I guess so. As long as you say it's from *you*, and not from me."

Then something happened that got everybody's attention. Keisha stopped worrying about whether she would remember all her lines for the play, Megan momentarily lost interest in her mural, Annie was distracted from worrying about her grandpa, and Bernadette stopped feeling left out, because on the Monday before the science fair, a sign went up on the front door of Garden Road Elementary School. ***SCIENCE FAIR UNFAIR!*** it declared, in bold red letters. Who would write such a thing? What could it mean? Nobody knew.

On Tuesday a different sign appeared, this one listing all kinds of facts about the school. For example:

1. It takes the same number of steps to walk around the *outside* of the school as to go through the front entrance, past the office, down the kindergarten hall, upstairs to the music room, back down to the gym and out the garage door.
2. The shortest tree in the yard is approximately half the height of the tallest one, but the widest tree is five times wider than the skinniest one.
3. The number of windows in the building is exactly the same as the number of tables in the lunchroom.
4. The number of classrooms, plus the number of teachers, multiplied by ten, equals the number of students in the school.

After reading this poster, lots of kids were counting and measuring all sorts of things at school—bricks, desks, water fountains—and the

Lunch Bunch came up with a new layout for the library to create space for two more computer stations. Ms. Chin was so impressed by their hard work she brought them homemade cookies and pink lemonade.

Wednesday, a third sign revealed that:

1. Ten boys (including Jackie Renfrew) would have tried out for the school choir if they'd known other boys were doing it.
2. Six girls (including Annie Wang) would have tried out for the soccer team if they'd known other girls were doing it.
3. All the kids polled liked carrot sticks for lunch but nobody liked whole carrots.
4. More kids got sent to the office on Friday than on any other day. (The writer wasn't sure whether this was because the kids really misbehaved more, or just that teachers were less patient at the end of the week.)

5. Although everyone said they hated strict teachers (like Mrs. Hawthorn) most wished that the easygoing ones had quieter classrooms (like Mrs. Hawthorn did).

These facts inspired the children to ask all sorts of questions, and they discovered some amazing things. Amelia Fisher in Grade Five realized that she was related to Terry Fisher in Grade Two, who was her mother's third cousin's son and had exactly the same dimple in his chin as she did. And Kim Pham connected the nasty rash on his hands with his turn as blackboard monitor.

Thursday morning there was a traffic jam outside Garden Road Elementary School. Even the kids who were normally late, the ones who finished their homework while getting dressed and ate their breakfast in the car, got to school on time because they wanted to read the new poster. It said that:

1. Mr. McGregor, the gym teacher, always made the first class of the day do sit-ups when he had been stuck in traffic, but gave them free play if he'd arrived at school early enough for an extra cup of coffee.
2. Ms. Chin never wore the same earrings twice in one week.
3. Mr. Cornell, the custodian, swept the halls in opposite directions on alternate days.
4. Mrs. Garcia always said *"Bonjour"* on Monday's announcements, *"Buenos Días"* on Tuesday, *"Kali Mera"* on Wednesday, *"Namaste"* on Thursday, and "Howdy, folks" on Friday.

So the students started studying the staff, and they learned all kinds of neat stuff. Nobody had realized before that the secretary had been a competitive figure skater, or that the new Grade Two teacher played drums in a rock band, or even that Mr. Cornell was a fantastic magician.

On Friday, the day of the science fair, there was nothing interesting at all on the front door of Garden Road Elementary School. Nothing but directions for visitors and the usual notices forbidding smoking and dogs on school property (or smoking dogs on school property). Everyone was as glum as the sole of an old sneaker until morning announcements, when Mrs. Garcia said "Howdy, folks," on the loudspeaker, and invited the whole school to visit the science fair in the gym at ten o'clock.

The gym was packed. The audience was surprised to discover that somehow Ngoc had managed to grow parsley in a pot full of coffee grounds, an achievement that earned him third prize, which was a purple ribbon and a fifteen-dollar gift card for books. They laughed at Alexandra's pet turtles, Bubble and Squeak, who made their way slowly but surely through a maze, winning her a blue ribbon for second prize, and a twenty-dollar gift card. And they admired Shamar's wonderful machine, which blew multi-colored bubbles around the gym. The university professors all agreed that he should win first prize of a red ribbon and a scientific calculator, as well as a chance to compete in the city finals. But the gym suddenly got silent when Mrs. Garcia asked for everybody's attention and called a fourth student up to the stage.

"Would Bernadette Inez O'Brian Schwartz from Mrs. Hawthorn's Grade Three class please join me on the stage?"

"Why me?" asked Bernadette.

"You're not the only one who's been observing things around here, young lady! Mrs. Hawthorn noticed how much time you spent writing in your notebook, so she suspected that *you* were the one responsible for those posters on the front door. Was she right?"

Her mother had told her never to lie, and

everyone says that you should always listen to your mother. So Bernadette confessed.

"Yes, it was me. Am I in trouble?"

She was trembling a little and trying not to cry, and she was already plotting revenge on Mrs. Hawthorn. She would expose her horrible teacher's secrets to the whole wide world. All the kids would laugh when they learned that Mrs. Hawthorn had once walked around school all day without realizing that there was pink bubble gum stuck to the back of her skirt! And that she was afraid of spiders! And that even though she was the oldest teacher in the entire school, she didn't know how to drive a car!

"No," said the principal, laughing.

"Pardon?" asked Bernadette.

"No, you're not in trouble at all. In fact, everyone has really enjoyed your investigations. And you've taught us a very good lesson about science too. Science isn't just about inventing things, or growing things, or exploding things. Science is mostly about paying attention to the world around us. You don't need fancy equipment like telescopes or microscopes to be a scientist. You just need a curious mind, a notebook, and a pencil. Or perhaps a whole *box* of pencils."

And with that, Mrs. Hawthorn came up and gave Bernadette a big hug, and a box of colored pencils, and a beautiful journal with a real leather cover. On the cover of the journal it said *Science Fair ~ Special Prize* in gold letters, followed by her name, *Bernadette Inez O'Brian Schwartz*, with all four parts spelled correctly (which, in Bernadette's experience, was quite unusual). And then Mrs. Hawthorn, who was grinning almost as much as Bernadette herself, made a little speech.

"Thank you, Bernadette. Your determination and love of science has persuaded Garden Road Elementary School that junior students like you should be allowed to participate in our science fair, even if you're not allowed into the city finals. In fact, we're creating this new award especially for someone from Kindergarten to Grade Three, and it will be given to a deserving student every year from now on."

As soon as Mrs. Hawthorn had finished speaking, the audience exploded with applause.

"Three cheers for Bernadette Inez O'Brian Schwartz," cried Jackie Renfrew. "A very talented scientist and a very good friend."

Bernadette bowed to Jackie, and then she did a silly chicken dance around the stage, waving her box of rainbow pencils and her spiffy new journal above her head, while Megan, Keisha, and Annie cheered. She couldn't believe it. She had actually won an award for science after all! And everyone was cheering for her! And even though Jasmine had gone away, she had so many friends!

"Thank you, Mrs. Hawthorn," she said. "And thank you too, Mrs. Garcia. You know what? I really think that Grade Three is going to be the best year *ever*!

The end